MONSTERS
IN THE GARDEN

Story and Pictures by Christopher Brook

Andersen Press • London

I used to be scared of the night.

I would cuddle Caruso, my cat, hoping that if I held him close he would keep me safe from the monsters in the garden.

Every night I heard sniffs, snuffles, snorts, snarls and haunting hoots and howls from outside in the darkness. And if I ran to Mum, she always said, "It's only the wind. Go back to bed."

But from my window, I could see dark shadows prowling around in the moonlight and sitting in the trees, with ghostly shapes flying overhead. I would jump back into bed and hold Caruso close beneath the covers.

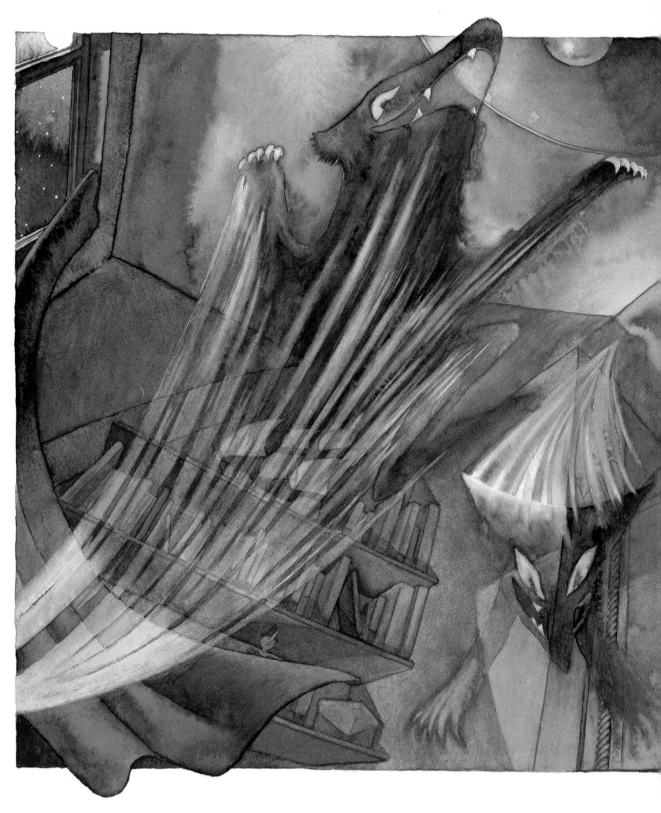

Even sleeping did no good, for in my dreams the
monsters all flew in through windows, doors and walls.

I used to think they would get me. I would lie
there trembling, until daylight sent them away.
But I knew they would be back!

Then one day, Caruso disappeared.

"I bet those monsters took him while
I was asleep," I said to Gran.
She smiled and told me not to worry.
"We'll find him," she said.

But he wasn't in the house,

he wasn't in the garden,

and nobody in our street had seen him.

We looked for him in the park, calling, "Caruso!
Caruso!" until at last I noticed it was getting dark.
I had been so worried that I had forgotten to be scared!
Suddenly I heard a grunt and then a snuffle.
I listened hard. I could hear noises all around me.

Now I was frightened! I shut my eyes as something
moved towards us.
"Oh, look!" whispered Gran.
So I opened them again. The dark shapes came
closer and I saw...

...three short, hairy, browny-grey creatures with long noses and black and white painted faces.
"They're badgers," said Gran.
"They're beautiful," I whispered back.

We watched them playing until they snuffled and
shuffled out of sight. Not monsters at all, but
clumsy, shy and lovely beasts.

We continued our search for Caruso and, as we walked,
Gran helped me to name all the noises. Snuffles,
sniffs, squeaks and screeches became rabbits, foxes ...

...bats and owls.

"They're all afraid of people, you see," said Gran.

"So they daren't come out in daylight."

"And I was scared of *them*," I said. We both laughed.

But then I remembered Caruso. We called him
again, but he still didn't come. I wanted to cry as I
thought of him lost and alone.

Then, as we turned into our street, a noise rose up and
filled the night. A noise far worse than anything I'd
heard before. It was a mournful, ghostly wail and it
was coming from *our* roof! Even Gran was scared.

Mum came running with a torch and neighbours
crowded round to see the monster that had
woken them.

The following night, as I cuddled Caruso, I thought of all I'd seen.

"The only frightening thing was you," I said. "You little monster." He purred and curled up safely in my arms.

And we both love the night time now.

10   9   8   7   6   5   4   3   2   1

British Library Cataloguing in Publication Data available.
ISBN 0 86264 577 8
This book has been printed on acid-free paper